Anxiety High Volume 1: There is Nothing Wrong with You!

David Boroughs, Joshua Boroughs

Copyright © 2023 by Introverts and Belonging LLC

Written By David Boroughs and Joshua Boroughs

Illustrated by David Boroughs

All rights reserved.

No portion of this book may be reproduced in any form without written permission from the publisher or author, except as permitted by U.S. copyright law.

Published 2023, Introverts and Belonging LLC, Houston, TX.

https://introvertsandbelonging.com/

Paperback ISBN: 979-8-9868562-3-0

eBook ISBN: 979-8-9868562-2-3

Library of Congress Control Number: 2023919772

The Anxiety High Book Series is a work of fiction. All content including people, names, characters, businesses, organizations, institutions, places, events, and incidents are from the authors' imaginations or used fictitiously. All resemblances to actual people, living or dead, events, or locals is coincidental.

This book was written and illustrated by humans, without the aid of AI.

To the parents and kids that find the courage, trust, patience, and love to team up and do something they have never done before.

Contents

1. Monday   1
2. Tuesday   22
3. Wednesday   41
4. Thursday   72
5. Friday   97
6. Acknowledgements   115
7. About the Authors   116
8. Notes   118

Monday

7:00 AM: Nyles's Home

"Beep! Beep! Beep! Beep!"

Slowly, Nyles opened his tired eyes and peeked out from under his pillow. The slim, blond high school Junior with a distinguishing gap between his front teeth groaned to himself "Why is it so hard to get out of bed!" Nyles reached for his phone, tempted to press the snooze feature, but chose to silence the alarm instead.

Two text messages already. They were both from Sam. It was student council election week, and she was nervous about her big speech. At Jane Piety Academy—or as the students referred to it, Anxiety High—the student council president candidates chose someone to introduce them to the student body (no one could really remember why). Sam had asked Nyles. Public speaking was not his thing, but he agreed to do it because Sam was one of his closest friends. Nyles only had a few close friends, but that was how he liked it.

> Did u get a draft of the intro finished

> Can we go over it today

> Yeah and sure after lunch in the library

> Thanks SO much see u later

Nyles reluctantly crawled out of bed and headed downstairs for breakfast. As he stepped into the hall, he could smell freshly baked cinnamon rolls. They were one of his dad's go-to meals since he had retired and taken over many of the household duties while his mom continued to work. The cinnamon rolls were easy for his dad to make because they came from a can, but Nyles was tired of them and didn't have the heart to tell his dad.

"Morning buddy!" said Nyles's dad.

"Hey," Nyles sat down at the kitchen table, where in addition to his cinnamon roll, Nyles saw vitamins, bacon ("protein for a growing young man" his mom liked to say), and a pile of fresh blueberries that his mom also insisted be on Nyles's breakfast plate.

"Do you have a tough schedule this week?"

"Same old s…"

"Stuff," Nyles's dad interrupted him.

"Thanks Dad," Nyles replied quickly, forcing a smile. "I was just going to say studying!" His dad returned the smile adding, "just making sure you aren't picking up bad habits from your mom and me."

In reality, Nyles was dreading the week. He had a nervous feeling that he couldn't shake. In addition to introducing Sam at the student council election assembly, today he had a round table discussion in history. Nyles hated these discussions because he never could get a word in edgewise. He despised interrupting people; it was a huge energy drain. Most of all, Nyles never liked that a substantial portion of his grade was based on his ability to compete verbally with his classmates.

After finishing his breakfast (covertly dumping his vitamins in the disposal because he hated the taste of the adult vitamins and longed for the days of the sugar coated chewables), Nyles headed back upstairs to finish getting ready for the day.

8:15 AM: Jane Piety Academy Courtyard

"Vote for Sam!"

Sam Silversmith repeated the words for what must

have been the hundredth time this morning. She was determined to win this year's student council president election.

"Hey Kelly! Don't forget to vote for me on Thursday!" she yelled to her friend who was heading to the cafeteria.

Kelly looked back and shouted, "I've got you girl!"

Sam had decided to run for the office of vice-president as a Junior. But her sister Sally, who was 10 years older, had encouraged her to run for president. "Vice-president? If it was me, I would just run for president. If you're going to do all the work to campaign, you might as well go for the whole enchilada!" Sally had been privately coaching Sam, specifically on how to stand out for the past couple of years. She had learned the importance of self-advocacy early in her career, the hard way, and wanted Sam to be more prepared than she had been.

At first Sam had dismissed the idea of running for president. She thought there was no way an underclassman could win and assumed the president had to be a Senior. To her surprise, though, when she looked at the school handbook there was no class requirement for student council officers and the current Senior candidate, Mark, was running unopposed. So, Sam made the bold decision to go for it!

She wanted the experience to show leadership on her college applications, but as she developed her campaign platform Sam decided to focus on helping Jane Piety Academy become more inclusive of students from diverse backgrounds. Sam's dad was Black, and her mom was from Mexico. She never knew what box to check on those optional ethnicity survey questions. Black or Hispanic didn't feel right because Sam always felt she was betraying one of her parents and she hated the idea of the "other" category when there was no multi-racial choice.

Sam had been curious to see how inclusive student leadership had been at the school and searched through years of Piety yearbooks. She wasn't surprised to learn that there had only been two female student council presidents at Jane Piety and as far as she could tell from low quality yearbook photos no Black or Latina students had held the office in the last 10 years. Sam decided to make this the focus of her campaign. "Vote Silversmith for a more inclusive school!" she shouted as she handed flyers to students as they arrived for the day.

Sam was a straight A student. She probably wouldn't be considered the smartest student at school, but many would agree, she might have been the hardest working. Good grades, well actually, perfect grades, were extremely important to Sam's parents because they knew how hard it was for underrepresented groups, "gente de color mija," as her mother would say, to compete in the professional world.[1] They loved Sam, and at the same time put tremendous pressure on her to perform academically in addition to, speaking perfect English. When Sam told them she was running for student council, they supported the idea but didn't want it to distract Sam from her studies—especially at Jane Piety Academy which was known for its high academic standards. Sam committed to keeping her grades up and for extra measure, emphasized how good student council would look on her college resume.

Nyles snuck up behind Sam, interrupting her thoughts. "What are you doing?" he asked.

His sudden appearance startled her, "Ay Dios mio! Not cool Nyles!" she scolded, then laughed in relief.[2] "Here, help me hand out the rest of these flyers."

Nyles welcomed the distraction and took half. Although not nearly as vocal as Sam, Nyles used the strategy of focusing on people he already knew and asking them to help distribute flyers as well. As a group, they managed to distribute them all before their first period bell.

11:45 AM: Jane Piety Academy History Class

It was finally time for the class Nyles had been dreading all weekend. He disliked history primarily because of the frequent discussions, but also because he found the class extremely boring. The absolute worst part for him was the fact that his teacher didn't understand him at all, nor did he try to. Today's class involved one of those "frequent discussions," which meant that Nyles had to somehow find a way to add to the conversation or his grade would suffer.

As soon as Nyles entered the classroom, he started to get nervous chills. The classroom was devoid of decorations. Mr. Cobb, with his thin white hair and a habit of looking over the rim of his glasses, had been teaching for years and was known for being blunt and putting as little effort as possible into his work. As a result, simply setting foot into the classroom was suffocating for someone like Nyles because the space essentially displayed what he perceived as the teacher's hostility.

Since it was still early in the year, Mr. Cobb didn't know everyone's name yet and had to do a traditional roll call. He went down the list in a normal fashion until he got to Nyles's name.

"Is Nyles River present today?" As usual, Mr. Cobb smirked and used an odd broken British accent he reserved only for Nyles.

Everyone else always giggled when this happened, no matter how many times they heard it. In this class, the students needed any entertainment they could get.

"Here." It was a bad start to what Nyles already knew would be a challenging class, but he tried his best to brush it off and stay focused on the discussion ahead.

After the teacher finished with roll call, he got on with explaining the assignment for the day, which was going to be a graded Socratic seminar.

Mr. Cobb seemed to focus on the students who naturally talked more, as was evident by the energy and attention he gave to this group. Nyles was concerned he would likely be grading people based on how much they talked rather than the quality of what they talked about. It seemed obvious to Nyles that the kids who naturally talked more were the ones that thrived in this class.

The seminar would take place over a thirty-minute period covering the reading they were supposed to have done the night before. It was Nyles's personal goal to make five good points in that time. He had learned a hard lesson at the start of the school year when he was publicly embarrassed by Mr. Cobb for not being ready for the discussion (his focus the night before had been studying for a math test). His mom had suggested preparing his comments in advance, which he had started doing to avoid a repeat of the stress and anxiety he had previously felt. In a class with none of his friends, a challenging teacher, and a menacing aura, this wasn't going to be simple for him and he knew it.

It did not begin well.

"Why doesn't Silent River start us off?" a boy with a reputation for pressing other people's buttons suggested with a snicker. Silent River was a nick name Nyles had been recently given because he was hesitant to speak in class.

Mr. Cobb said nothing, and just looked at Nyles. Everyone

expected him to get flustered (as usual), but he was determined not to let this affect him, so he asked a thought-provoking opening question (one that he had prepped) and it led to a heated discussion.

After that, there were fewer opportunities for him to break into the conversation, but he managed to a few times, including an idea that was quickly mulled over then dismissed by the students that dominated these sessions. This disappointed him. Since this happened during every discussion, after class he tried to talk to Mr. Cobb about ways that he could get more integrated into the conversation (talking to his teachers was something his parents continually suggested). Unfortunately, the teacher was unapologetic as he refused to help Nyles at all.

"This is your problem, Nyles. You need to solve it on your own."

Nyles left the class feeling like he typically did after a group discussion—wondering what was wrong with him and why other people could talk with ease in groups, like it was no big deal.

1:15 PM: Jane Piety Academy Library

Nyles had agreed to meet with two of his friends during their free period, so they gathered in the library. They had found a small dark hidden alcove in the back corner that was always empty. It was a sanctuary of solitude in the middle of Anxiety High's chaos. Studying was often their stated intent, but more often than not they just vegged and hung out. And all Nyles wanted to do right now was chill and mess around.

"Math was sooooo boring today." Johnny complained as he sat down and took his computer out of his backpack. "I have no clue what's going on and the teacher isn't even trying to be helpful."

Nyles could sense that his intended goal of messing around was in jeopardy.

"Calmate Johnny. I understood the lesson," Sam said.[3] Let me see if I can clear up what's confusing you." Nyles could tell she was trying her best to help a friend despite the pressure she was under.

Reluctantly, Nyles added, "I know a thing or two about math. Show me what you're working on."

Sam gave him a grateful wink.

While Nyles and Johnny went over the math problems, Sam asked, "Nyles, how did your discussion go in history?"

Focused on the math problem, Nyles didn't answer right away. Finally, he looked up and saw she was waiting for an answer. "What? Oh, history. It was meh—" In all honesty, he was barely satisfied with the results, but wanting to seem more positive he added, "I was actually able to get in a lot more points than I thought I would."

A few minutes later, Johnny threw down his pencil in frustration. "Remind me when the election is? It would be great if it's during my next math class."

"Thursday at 2:30," Sam and Nyles both responded in unison. Everyone laughed.

Johnny looked between his two friends. "What are you two, secret identical twins? Anyhow, how are your speeches coming along?"

Nyles and Sam were both pretty much done writing them and they both shared the same primary concern, that they wouldn't be confident enough talking in front of so many people.

Once again, they answered simultaneously. "I'm nervous," said Sam. "I'm good," said Nyles. He was nervous, too, but wasn't comfortable talking about it, not even with his closest friends.

Johnny laughed, "Maybe you're not as identical as I

thought." He glanced at his phone and yelped "I need to run. Thanks for the math help, Nyles. See you guys later." He grabbed his computer and dashed out of the alcove.

Sam and Nyles spent the rest of their free period reviewing each other's speeches. Afterward, Sam asked Nyles, "Are you really OK giving this speech?"

Nyles was still uneasy telling her the truth and said, "Uh, yeah, um, it's all good, no worries." He desperately needed a change of subject. "Hey look, Johnny forgot his calculator. Let me run it to him before class." He grabbed the calculator and shoved his speech in his backpack. With a quick "See you later," he rushed out of the secret alcove.

"That was weird," Sam muttered. Then she shrugged, packed up, and headed to her next class.

11:00 PM: Nyles's Home

"What was that!" Nyles yelled into his gaming headset. "I thought we were working together!" Johnny had just ambushed him in the latest online multi-player game that had been released.

"Too bad dude!" Johnny's voice boomed enthusiastically

from the headset.

Nyles laughed, "Who needs enemies when they have friends like you? Hey Johnny, it's getting late, I'll find you at school tomorrow."

"Later dude." Johnny's avatar disappeared from the screen. Nyles logged off the game and went to his room. He had left his phone on his bed and saw there was a new message from Sam.

> Are u still feeling confident about giving the speech

Nyles grabbed his phone, read the message, sighed, and then quickly typed a reply.

> I wasnt totally honest today with u

> Im actually really nervous

> Ik its important to u though so im trying my best to tough it out

Im really nervous too tbh

I couldnt tell by the way u were acting at school even though u said u were

Friend tip when a girl tells u something about herself listen and believe it

I only just started studying for our math test tomorrow because of how much I was focusing on the speech

Do u want to try and get some last minute studying together over facetime cuz I haven't studied much either

I was distracted too

Is that what u call playing video games with Johnny now

Yeah definitely facetime me

Nyles and Sam were both trying to focus so there wasn't much casual banter. The video call wasn't really necessary (Nyles's camera faced the ceiling, so Sam saw the occasional rotation of a fan blade; Sam's camera was pointed at her but only captured her right ear and its pearl earring), but they liked working together.

The only time either one spoke was when they had a question. Sam usually asked many more questions as Nyles tended to be quite gifted at science and math.

"Hey, can you help me with number 11 on the practice test por favor?" she asked.[4]

"Oh, I struggled a little with that problem, too, because there's a lot of information that you don't need. So basically, you want to start by trying to isolate X and then..." Nyles carefully went over each detail of the answer.

This continued for almost two hours until both Sam and Nyles had had about as much math as they could take.

After the call, they were both still a little nervous about the test, which was natural since this test score was worth ten percent of their final grade and they were distracted by the upcoming speech.

Regardless, they both tried to get some sleep, which wasn't easy because of the stress and anxiety that continued to build as election day drew closer.

Tuesday

7:00 AM: Nyles's Home

"Beep! Beep! Beep! Beep!"

Nyles was already awake. He hadn't gotten much sleep. He was so worried about the upcoming student council elections that he had been up reviewing and practicing his speech. He grabbed his phone and silenced the alarm.

Nyles had been working on his speech since he woke up at four in the morning. He had propped up his phone and hit the record button. The first time he tried it, Nyles forgot everything he was going to say almost instantly. Frustrated, he stopped the recording.

"Why is this so hard when there is no one else here?" he asked to the empty room.

Nyles decided to read his speech aloud without recording himself. That went fine. Then he tried reading it to the camera again. Things were going well until he stumbled on a word. Frustrated once again, he stopped the recording. Then he remembered a technique his mother had suggested.

"All I'm doing is reinforcing me stopping when I make a

mistake, and that is not what I want to be practicing. I can't stop recording until I'm finished. If I make a mistake, I just need to push on."

Nyles hit record. Once again, he read the speech aloud, but this time he made it to the end without stopping the recording.

"Progress!"

Then he watched it.

"This may not have been a good idea," Nyles worried. He felt weird watching himself on video.

But he continued and eventually had fifteen attempts. None were perfect, but there was improvement.

"I have more work to do," Nyles acknowledged.

It was now 7:00 AM and he was tired. Nyles jumped into the shower, quickly dressed, grabbed breakfast (a plain strawberry Pop-tart because his dad hated the ones with icing), and headed to school.

9:40 AM: Jane Piety Academy Auditorium

"Ringggggg."

The second period bell echoed through the hallways. Nyles packed up his honors calculus books and headed to the auditorium. Both student council president candidates, Mark and Sam, along with their introducing speakers were expected to meet with Mrs. Sweeney, the brand-new school principal, and a few other teachers to practice their upcoming speeches.

As Nyles approached the entrance to the auditorium, he heard Sam call from behind, "Hey Nyles, hold up!"

Nyles turned and saw Sam smiling at him.

"Como estas? Are you feeling any better today?" Sam greeted him.[5]

"I'm OK," Nyles replied. "How are you?"

Sam raised her eyebrows, "I've been feeling nervous all day about this practice. I barely slept thinking about it last night."

"Really?" Nyles responded. "You are such a great public speaker, why are you nervous?"

Sam looked around to ensure no one else could hear and then winked. "It's all an act, this stuff scares me to death."

Nyles had lied to Sam. He wasn't OK. In fact, he was close to panic as the time to practice the speech approached. But it made him feel a little better to know that he wasn't panicking alone.

As they entered the auditorium, Nyles noticed Mr. Cobb was one of the observers that Mrs. Sweeney had invited.

"What is he doing here?" Nyles thought.

Mr. Cobb didn't acknowledge Nyles as they walked past the history teacher and sat in the front row near Mark and Rory, Mark's pick to introduce him.

From what Nyles had heard, Mrs. Sweeney had recently returned to the United States after serving in a variety of administrative roles in small international schools designed for English-speaking students. She had short hair, a pleasant smile, round glasses, and often wore clothes with vibrant floral patterns. Mrs. Sweeney stepped up to the mic and tapped it to make sure it was on. *"Thump, thump, thump."* The sound echoed through the empty cavernous auditorium.

"Hello all and good morning! This shouldn't take long. I just wanted you to have an opportunity to practice your speeches in the venue. I've also asked a few teachers that happen to have this period free to sit in the audience and provide some feedback. Let's start with the candidates. Sam, why don't you go first then we'll give Mark a shot."

Sam looked at Nyles and whispered, "Wish me Luck." She got up and walked confidently onto the stage where she opened her speech, placed it on the podium, and adjusted the microphone. Sam took a deep breath, looked out over the empty room as if it was full of people and began her speech. She did an excellent job, even for practice, and only made a few mistakes while referencing her written words only a couple times. Sam had obviously been practicing. When she was done, Nyles, Mark, and Rory clapped along with the teacher observers.

Then Mrs. Sweeney approached the mic and said, "Nice job Sam. Loved the content and great delivery."

The teacher observers followed Mrs. Sweeney and provided overall positive comments.

Mark was next up. He approached the mic with vigor. Nyles noticed that he didn't have anything written down. Mark raised the mic up, smiled a Hollywood smile, and then proceeded to improvise an enthusiastic speech that flowed well and left Nyles wondering how anyone could possibly pull that off? "That was awesome," Nyles thought. "On the other hand, I am not sure what he just said!"

Mrs. Sweeney stood, complimented Mark, and opened the floor up to the teacher observers.

Mr. Cobb said, "Nice job Mark! It reminded me of some of your history debates!"

Only one teacher commented that his content would benefit from a more thought-out and meaningful message but ended the feedback with "Loved the gravitas!"

Mrs. Sweeney once again stood and approached the podium. "Rory, why don't you go next? Remember, you are just introducing the candidate, so no need to go overboard."

Rory approached the mic and started his practice session. Nyles didn't hear what Rory said or pay attention to his delivery. Nyles was focused on his own feelings. His heartbeat was accelerating, surrounding noises sounded like he was hearing them from inside a drum, his hands were sweating, shaking, and growing numb. Nyles tried to calm himself. He wiped his hands on his shorts and gently, repeatedly squeezed his fists to try and restore blood flow to fight the numbness.

"Mr. River?" Nyles heard someone say in the distance.

Rory was finished and had returned to his seat. Nyles felt Sam grab his hand. "Are you OK?" He looked at Sam, then Mrs. Sweeney and slowly stood.

As Nyles approached the stage, he stumbled up the stairs, which helped bring him back to his current terrifying reality. He continued walking, what seemed an endless distance, towards the podium.

Mrs. Sweeney put her hand over the mic and whispered, "Are you ready? Do you need some water?"

Nyles just stared back, slightly shook his head from side-to-side, and said, "I'm OK."

Mrs. Sweeney sat back down while Nyles opened his folded speech. He could feel his hands shaking as he opened the paper and was embarrassed because he thought everyone could tell how nervous he was. He managed to get it open and launched into a quiet and fast reading of the introduction. Nyles wasn't sure why he read it; he had practiced and memorized the short speech, but the words were just not materializing in his head. When he finished, Sam and another teacher provided some applause and a few encouraging words.

Mrs. Sweeney approached the podium and said, "Why don't we hear from our observers?"

The first teacher smiled and said, "I loved your words, but I had a hard time hearing you."

The second teacher chimed in, "I agree, and it might be helpful to slow down a bit."

Nyles knew they were both valid observations.

Mr. Cobb was less gentle with his remarks, "Nyles, no feedback from me. Sam, I do have some advice for you. Find someone else to introduce you." That was it. He stood up and walked out of the auditorium.

Mrs. Sweeney curiously watched Mr. Cobb march out, then looked at Nyles and said, "You may want to set up some time to talk with Counselor Austin and ask him about techniques to stay calm ahead of the live event on Thursday. And, of course, keep practicing!"

As Nyles left the stage, he saw Rory give Mark a big high five and say, "You've got this dude! No problem at all!"

He noticed Sam approaching and was surprised she was giving him a big smile. "Look Nyles, I know what you're going through. I have similar overwhelming feelings when I speak in public. It took me some time and the help of my sister to understand those feelings were going to be there regardless. That they were normal for me. So now, when I feel them, instead of worrying and trying to get them to go away, I just embrace my feelings as a warning sign that some uncomfortable stuff is about to go down. The audience has no idea what you are planning to say so just go with it and tell them how amazing I am!"

Nyles smiled. "Thanks Sam, that helps. I agree, you are amazing. Look I'll understand if you want to find someone else."

Sam interrupted him, "Heck no, I'm not letting you off that easy! You've got this! And there's no way we're going to give Mr. Cobb that satisfaction."

"Thanks again, I really appreciate your support," Nyles said. "But are these types of feelings really normal? It sure feels like there is something wrong with me."

"Of course, they're normal. Some of us are simply better at hiding them than others," Sam reassured him.

3:45 PM: Jane Piety Academy Counselor's Office

Nyles had a lot that he wanted to get off his chest, and

the school counselor had always been willing to help him out in the past, so he decided to take Mrs. Sweeney's suggestion and drop by after school to see if Counselor Austin had any free time.

He was mentally reliving the panic he had experienced at the practice session when his inner dilemma was interrupted by Counselor Austin calling out to him, "Hey Nyles, what brings you by?"

"Sorry for the unscheduled visit," Nyles mumbled, "but I was wondering if you had any time for me to discuss some things with you."

Even though the counselor had a tough time hearing him, he assumed Nyles needed to talk and invited him into his office.

Counselor Austin was in his early thirties, consistently wore sweater vests whether in the cold of winter or the heat of summer, had a goatee, and was easy to talk to. However, this time Nyles didn't know where to start, so he chose to rip off the proverbial bandage by saying, "Earlier today I ran through my practice speech introducing Sam for the student council election, but I totally messed it up! I was so nervous! If I'm that nervous with a few other people in the room, how am I going to handle the hundreds that will be there on Thursday? I can't screw this up for Sam!"

Counselor Austin tried to calm him down. "Hey, we've talked through similar concerns before, remember, regarding classes that require a lot of verbal participation? It's only natural to be nervous when it's your first-time speaking in a venue this big. That's a fear almost everyone has, whether they are naturally social or not."

"I still feel like something might be wrong with me, because I have that fear of talking in front of small groups as well," Nyles responded.

For the counselor, this was a common conversation at JPA. He explained to Nyles that there was nothing wrong with him, and said he thought people like Nyles struggled because our society is biased towards extroverted behaviors, which give outgoing, social people an advantage over those who prefer to pause and think before they speak.

"In most high schools it's common for students and teachers to think the popular and outgoing people represent 'normal' behavior, but what most people don't understand is that when it comes to personality type you can't define normality based on one example," the counselor explained. "Trust me, there is nothing wrong with you. You're good at math. Think about it this way. Personality type is represented by a bell-shaped distribution or curve with introverts on one side and extroverts on the other. Most people label introverts as 'quiet' while extroverts are admired for their 'social' skills, but the difference really lies with how each group manages stimulus and recharges their internal 'battery.' Nyles, you're not just good at math, aren't you on the advanced track?"

Nyles frustratedly said, "Yes, but what does that have to do with this?"

Counselor Austin gestured to him to remain calm and said, "Please bear with me. Do you know what the other name for a bell-shaped distribution is?"

Nyles looked to the side while thinking and then confidently stated, "It's sometimes called a normal distribution."

"Yes!" blurted out the counselor. "It's called a normal distribution because it takes all of the samples on the curve, in this case people's personality types, to reflect normality."

Nyles thought he understood but wanted more time and said, "Interesting, I'll probably need some time to think about that?"

Counselor Austin smiled and said, "Absolutely, take all the time you need. It's a difficult lesson for your age group to learn because there is so much societal pressure to fit in. It often takes people many years before they gain the confidence to accept that their uniqueness is not only normal, but also valued."

Nyles sighed and said, "I wish I had several years to figure this out, but the speech is this week. Is there something that will help me now?"

Counselor Austin smiled again and said, "You're right! You do need more immediate help. I will teach you some exercises that will help you calm down and mitigate your anxiety." The counselor talked to Nyles about and practiced several techniques like focused breathing and tried his best to reassure him.

"Thanks for your help. I'm still nervous, but hopefully your techniques will help me manage my feelings during my speech a little better now," Nyles said on his way out.

The talk had helped him. He still wasn't confident, but he did have a newfound hope based on the counselor's advice. As he exited the school to walk home, a cool breeze blew across his face, which was a welcome relief from what had been a scorching hot summer.

10:30 PM: Nyles's Home

As Nyles lay in his bed reading his text messages, he reflected on the day. He had intentionally avoided his parents because he wasn't ready to talk about the practice speech and he just wanted alone time. It had been brutal, but Sam's positive support and the talk with Counselor Austin had helped. He took a deep breath, held it for several seconds and then slowly released. He repeated. He noticed a message from Sam and responded.

> Do u feel ok after what happened during practice

> Yeah

> I went to see the counselor after school and he gave me some tips on how to calm down during the real thing

> K just remember that u r only the opener for my speech and there probably wont be that much attention on u

> Ik but I still have to survive our tests during the next couple days before I can even think about the speech anymore

Omg Ive been so hung up on the election Ive been slacking off on studying too

I have to ace them or my parents will be mad at me even if I win

Do you want to study during lunch tmr

Ill see u then

Wednesday

7:00 AM: Nyles's Home

"Beep! Beep! Beep! Beep!"

Once again, Nyles was wide awake today sitting at the small desk by his bed. This darn speech was going to be the death of him. "Why was public speaking always so hard for me? I guess we call Jane Piety Academy 'Anxiety High' for a reason," thought Nyles. He silenced the alarm from his smart watch.

"Looking on the bright side, one good thing about waking up so early is that I was able to spend some more time reviewing for my calculus and Spanish tests!" he thought. "The review later with Sam will help as well." He looked at his schedule on his phone and saw that he had history and Mr. Cobb to look forward to after lunch. "I'd rather study for tests any day than attend that class," Nyles said aloud to his empty room.

8:00 AM: Jane Piety Academy Entrance

"Mr. Cobb! Mr. Cobb!" shouted Mrs. Sweeney as they were approaching the teacher's entrance. Mr. Cobb slowly turned and acknowledged the school's principal with a slight wave.

"Good morning, Principal Sweeney, how can I help you?" stated Mr. Cobb as the fit administrator jogged up to him in her sneakers.

"Do you have a couple of minutes? I want to discuss your feedback at yesterday's dry run speeches."

Anticipating a lecture from the school administrator, Mr. Cobb automatically grimaced when he heard the request. He pulled himself together and said "Sure, is it ok to speak in my classroom?" Mrs. Sweeney nodded in agreement and followed. Upon entering the history classroom, she noticed how institutional it felt. There was literally nothing on the walls, really no way of even knowing it was a history class and if it hadn't been for the traditional desks, a classroom at all. Mrs. Sweeney shook off the observation and got straight to the point. "Mr. Cobb, I think everyone respects your unbridled honesty and we know we can always rely on you to express your opinion, but I think you may have lost sight of the fact that you were there to help the students yesterday and..."

Mr. Cobb interrupted Mrs. Sweeney and defensively

replied, "I did just that! And if you are referring to Sam Silversmith, I gave her the best advice I could at the time, what I thought was in her best interest."

Mrs. Sweeney sighed. "There is no doubt you told Sam what you thought would help, but you totally ignored your responsibility to help Nyles as well. In fact, the way you handled that was potentially devastating to the young man."

Mr. Cobb slowly shook his head and gave the administrator a defiant stare. "Look, I have Nyles in my class, and he has a problem. He is too quiet. He doesn't have the courage to put himself out there, to take risks around others."

It was the principal's turn to shake her head. "Mr. Cobb, with all due respect, whether you realize it or not, it is your job to assess the needs and help all your students grow and thrive in an environment that leverages their strengths. Have you ever considered you may have an unconscious bias against introverted kids and that your in-class discussion may not support their learning style? Do you understand that you may unintentionally show favor towards extroverted kids because of this?"

Mr. Cobb looked a little shocked. "Mrs. Sweeney, I treat

all my students the same. They must learn to fight for themselves! You know that you can't create diamonds without pressure, and I provide them the pressure that will prepare them for the real world."

Mrs. Sweeney responded, "Yeah, but that same pressure sometimes causes earthquakes. Did you ever consider that some kids thrive in your homogeneous environment while other kids struggle?"

Mr. Cobb started to reply but Mrs. Sweeney quickly said, "Don't answer. Look, there has been some early student and parent feedback that some students have a difficult time in your class, and until now I haven't acted on it because I didn't understand where it came from. But based on yesterday and this conversation, it could be because the classroom culture that you have created favors the students who are naturally better public speakers and makes it harder for the rest. I understand that you are not doing this consciously and have good intentions, but it must change. I will speak to Counselor Austin and have him contact you about developing strategies to create a classroom where all your students feel like they belong. Can you agree to this course of action?"

Mr. Cobb, in pure disbelief, looked at Mrs. Sweeney with a blank expression and said, "Yes ma'am," while simultaneously thinking that he hated breaking in new principals.

1:30 PM: Jane Piety Academy History Class

The bell rang and Nyles quickly scarfed down the rest

of his greasy, tasty cafeteria cheeseburger and headed to history. This was Nyles's least favorite rotation on his class schedule because he had Mr. Cobb's history class three times in one week.

"I get nothing out of these history classes," Nyles thought. "I would be better off just reading the textbook. It would definitely be less stressful!"

Nyles slipped into the class right before the bell rang, since he didn't want to spend any more time than was needed in the medieval dungeon that Mr. Cobb had managed to create. He quickly found his desk.

Like clockwork: Roll call, weird accent, student laughter.

Remembering a corny comedy movie from the early 1990's his parents made him watch one time about a person who relived the same day repeatedly, Nyles silently screamed to himself, "I'm stuck in a perverted version of *Groundhog Day*!"

Mr. Cobb finished his administrative duties then stood up, walked to the front of his desk, and leaned back on it. He looked like he was searching for the right words. Then sighed and blurted out, "I have been told that my methods may be too tough for some of you. Instead of learning about the rise of fascism in the early 20th century today, we are going to talk about what we can change to make our discussions better. Does anyone have any ideas?"

Nyles noticed a few hands shoot up. It was the kids that typically dominated the conversations in the classroom, the ones who always confidently expressed their ideas without hesitation.

Nyles thought, "If only I had been programmed that way."

Mr. Cobb pointed at Sue, "Yes, Miss Barns what do you think?"

Sue, one of the school's debate team captains, said, "I think we waste too much time debating different ideas when we usually have a great idea in the first few minutes. If we focus on the early ideas, we would be able to dive deeper into the few that really matter to the group."

Nyles wanted to interject but couldn't. In his opinion, "If the early ideas were wrong, we would be potentially wasting the entire discussion time!"

Mr. Cobb said, "Thanks Miss Barns. Any other thoughts?" Sue automatically put her hand back up as he moved to the next student.

The conversation continued between Mr. Cobb and the "dominant few."

Nyles raised his hand but wasn't called on and when he tried to express a counter opinion by interrupting, which was still very hard for him to do, he was immediately drowned out by someone else. Nyles had ideas, he just felt like it was futile to express them because no one was going to listen. He gradually focused more and more on his internal conversation and lost track of the class's progress.

Just then, Nyles was pulled back to reality from his inner world.

"Mr. River. Mr. River. Mr. River!" Mr. Cobb repeated trying to get his attention.

"Yes, Mr. Cobb?" replied an embarrassed Nyles as his heart raced.

"I was wondering what our quiet students had to think about the subject. Do you care to add value to our conversation?" Mr. Cobb said as he slowly waved his arm around the room gesturing to the rest of the students.

Nyles could hear his pulse increasing. He could sense panic and was struggling to understand why Mr. Cobb had just labeled him as a "quiet" student. Nyles thought, "Quiet! He might as well just have said, 'Silent River, do you have any value to add?'" Thoughts continued to swirl in Nyles's active mind, "Why 'quiet,' why not 'thoughtful' or 'insightful'? I'll always be seen as the 'quiet kid'!"

Nyles felt a nudge in his back and heard the kid behind him say "Cat got your tongue Silent River?"

Mr. Cobb didn't hear the exchange, but did sense something was going on and said, "Mr. Jones, please leave Mr. River alone. Well, Mr. River, do you care to share your wisdom?"

The classroom was completely silent.

Nyles continued to panic internally. Externally, he could feel the sweat on his forehead and sense the reddening of his face. He then said, "I have ideas."

Mr. Cobb immediately interrupted and said, "Great, then let's hear them!"

Nyles cleared his throat and said, "I would benefit from more time to think about topics before speaking about them. Take this specific topic for example. I know there is a lot we can do to improve our discussions, but I tend to come up with better solutions when I have time alone to think."

"Really?" said Mr. Cobb, who was skeptical because, except for this instance, he always provided the discussion topics at least one day in advance.

"Ringgggggg." The end of period bell sounded.

Mr. Cobb shouted over the bell, "Ok, it looks like Mr. River has assigned everyone homework. Please write down three to five suggestions for making our discussions better and email your lists to me by midnight."

Nyles, feeling like a truck just unexpectedly hit him, slowly packed up his books. As he got up, someone bumped him back into his desk and said, "Thanks for the extra homework Silent River!"

2:45 PM: Jane Piety Academy Courtyard

During that afternoon's free period, Nyles sat in the courtyard typing the email that Mr. Cobb had assigned to the class while wondering how honest he could be in the note. He was exhausted by the teacher and the class and just wanted to feel like he belonged. With a great deal of hesitancy, Nyles started to type. He then deleted, typed some more, and then deleted again. This internal debate went on for a while until Nyles had a draft note.

Mr. Cobb,

Here is my feedback on how to make history class and the discussion in it more inclusive.

First, as I said in class, providing notice in advance helps students like me who need time to think about things to formulate their answers. Usually, you do a good job of this, giving us at least a day's notice on all history discussion topics. When I have this notice, I prepare several discussion points ahead and try and make sure I verbalize them during the discussion. Today, I did not have this luxury and was busy trying to gather my thoughts when you called on me. Even though the class may have blamed me for the assignment today, balancing the numerous discussions with more written assignments like this one would be helpful to the students that prefer writing over talking.

Today when you called on me, I think you were trying to include me in the conversation. Thank you for that, but the way you did it made it harder for me to contribute. Why did you choose to label me as "quiet" instead of just simply asking what I thought? This would have helped me feel useful instead of like someone who is wasting everybody's

time. So please, when you see someone who needs help breaking into a conversation, help them. Just do it in a way that makes them feel like they belong in the conversation.

Next, as the teacher and discussion facilitator you can help ensure that the class learns all the key lessons from a discussion. Sometimes, it will take a while to get all the key points out and if the group spends all their time discussing the first couple of things that are said, they may never learn the right lessons. Please help the class move to new subjects when they seem stuck on a less important one, even if the class's discussion is vibrant and active.

Finally, I would appreciate it if you would not use the accent when you say my name during roll call. I am not sure why you do it. It further alienates me from my classmates and I think contributes to the nicknames they are using. Yes, my name is novel, but it is my name.

Nyles River

The closing paragraph was not part of the homework request, but re-living today's class had ignited a spark in Nyles. He decided that there was no better time than the present to highlight the teacher's unwanted behavior. Nyles re-read the email a few times. He then closed his eyes, took a deep breath, and hit send. Panic and relief simultaneously spread through him as the message disappeared into cyberspace.

3:30 PM: Jane Piety Academy Counselor's Office

Mrs. Sweeney was nearing Counselor Austin's office when a young student exited.

"I don't know her," thought the principal. "I wonder if that is because she's a new student or because I'm the new principal?"

The student looked back in the counselor's office and said, "I knew that 'Anxiety High' was a tough school, but I had no idea it would be this difficult!"

Mrs. Sweeney heard the counselor reply from inside his office, "What you are feeling is not unusual for our new students. Hang in there and come see me whenever you want to talk."

"Looks like we are both new," laughed Mrs. Sweeney to herself and then immediately wondered, "Anxiety High?"

After the student had hurried down the hallway towards the first-year lockers, the principal stuck her head in Counselor Austin's door and knocked on the door frame.

"Mrs. Sweeney, so nice to see you, please come in. To what do I owe this pleasure?" said Mr. Austin with a smile.

"Thank you," said the school principal as she entered, closed the door, and sat across from him.

Mrs. Sweeney admired the counselor's exotic and colorful photos, many of the locations she had seen firsthand during her time abroad. She had a master's degree in school administration with an undergraduate degree in psychology. Her secret passion was understanding why people act the way they do, and she often wondered why she didn't become a counselor or therapist. But she knew that it was important to not overstep her role and let her team manage their areas of expertise.

"I had a conversation with Mr. Cobb and I would like you to meet with him, tomorrow if possible, and talk about his behaviors," said Mrs. Sweeney in a matter-of-fact way. "But before we dive into that discussion, what is this 'Anxiety High'?"

Counselor Austin, with a look of surprise on his face, said, "No one told you that many of the kids, a lot of the parents, and even some of the teachers refer to this fine institution as 'Anxiety High'?"

With a serious and concerned look, Mrs. Sweeney replied "No."

"Well," the counselor continued, "I guess it's because it rhymes with our name, Jane Piety. Piety, anxiety. And the school is known for being particularly challenging and stressful, both academically and socially. The nickname has been around as long as I have been here. I've heard on more than one occasion we used to have a principal who would say, 'Can't make diamonds without pressure' when students and parents alike would talk about the demands of the school on the students."

"Interesting, that's the second time today that I have been educated about diamond creation," quipped Mrs. Sweeney. "Please schedule some time on my calendar so we can discuss the mental health of our school family. Based on what sounds like a well-earned nickname, we probably have some work to do."

Counselor Austin nodded. "Sure thing."

"Now to the reason I stopped by," Mrs. Sweeney said. "I need your help with Mr. Cobb..."

6:00 PM: Nyles's Home

Wednesday nights were always special for Nyles. For as

long as he could remember, his grandparents would join their family for dinner. Nyles loved G-Pa and G-Ma, as he had recently started referring to them. It was a shift from Grandpa and Grandma that he had tried one evening and to his delight they seemed to adore the new, younger version of their tried-and-true names.

"How's it going G-Pa?" said Nyles entering the living room.

"Hey Nyles, it's going well. You'll never hear me complain about getting time to visit with you and the family," Nyles's grandpa replied. "More importantly, how are you and how is school going?"

Nyles hesitated and then said, "School is school G-Pa. There are some good days and some harder ones."

Grandpa could sense (using his G-Pa superpowers) that Nyles was holding something back. "I get it, high school is a strange dichotomy. It can be the best time of your life while simultaneously being the worst. I think we all experience it, but as adults we forget how hard it can be at times. Are you struggling with anything right now?"

Nyles thought, "G-Pa must be able to read minds, or at least faces and body language!" He shook his head and looked down.

Grandpa said, "Hey, this is a safe space, you can talk to me without fear of judgement."

"Thanks G-Pa, this has been a tough week for me. I don't like being the center of attention and this week I've struggled with being heard in history and at the same time I agreed to help Sam by introducing her as a student council president candidate at the school assembly." Nyles continued, "And to top it off, I was given a nickname recently by one of the kids which has caught on with others and spread like wildfire. They're calling me 'Silent River.'"

Grandpa thought about this for a moment and said, "Do you think they're doing it because of your introverted nature?"

Nyles said, "I've heard you talk to Mom and Dad about introversion before, but I really am not 100% sure what it means even though Counselor Austin tried to explain it today."

"Well admitting your confusion is better than most people who typically assume they understand personality types when they really don't," said Grandpa. "You come from a long line of introverted people—me, your G-Ma, your mom, and your dad all lean towards the introverted end of the personality spectrum. Most assume that it means a person is shy, or they can't speak in public, or in some cases people think introversion is a personality flaw that just needs fixing. They are all wrong."

Nyles interrupted, "I get labeled as the 'quiet' kid quite often which is probably where the new nickname is coming from."

Grandpa smiled and shook his head in acknowledgment then continued, "While it is true that many introverts do come across as quiet, it is because introverts usually need to absorb and think about things before they speak about them. And often this may take some time. If you put an introvert on the spot and expect them to give an immediate answer, you may not get their best work. Introverts typically need a little quiet time in a low stimulus environment to think."

Nyles blurted, "I tried to tell Mr. Cobb that very thing today!"

Grandpa went on to say, "The good news is that introverts, like you, often come up with brilliant solutions to hard-to-solve problems so it would be wise for Mr. Cobb to listen to you." G-Pa then refocused the discussion, "Introverts lose energy when around others or in highly stimulating environments, while extroverts thrive in this space. Conversely, extroverts lose energy when alone or during times of low stimulation. When this happens, people naturally seek out the environment that allows them to recharge. For you, it is a quiet spot by yourself."

Nyles thought about this for a while, and G-Pa let it soak in.

"Maybe that's why they are calling me 'Silent River,' because as an introvert I lose energy in group settings and gravitate to quiet places to recharge. I just thought there was something wrong with me."

Grandpa replied, "Just wait one-minute young man. If you don't take anything else away from this conversation, listen to me now! There is nothing wrong with you! I spent much of my early engineering career believing there was something wrong with me just because of my personality type. It took me a long time, a lot of deep personal reflection, and help from some great friends and leaders, to understand that both introversion and extroversion are normal personality types and about half of all people share a similar preference as you and me. Do you think there is something wrong with half of the population just because they prefer to think about things before talking about them?"

Nyles smiled, "When you put it like that, I guess I am

really no different than the other introverted kids at my school. We are all in the same boat. Sam is one of my closest friends, and she has similar preferences to me. She's awesome—there is definitely nothing wrong with her!"

Grandpa smiled. "I was thinking about that nickname. Do they know that Nyles is your grandfather's name on your mom's side? That you are named after him as a sign of respect and your first name has nothing to do with your current last name or the famed river in Africa?"

Nyles said, "No, I don't think they care."

G-Pa chuckled, "You're probably right. I bet you didn't know that your great-great grandfather River was named Tennessee. Yep, Tennessee River!"

Nyles laughed and said, "I had no idea."

G-Pa went on, "Everyone thought he was named after the actual Tennessee River, but he wasn't. He was named after a racehorse called Tennessee Victory. That is right, your great-great grandfather's name on his birth certificate was Tennessee Victory River!"

Nyles continued to laugh as he thought about this

revelation.

G-Pa said, "But back to the issue at hand. Have you ever spent any time on a large river?"

Nyles almost immediately perked up and said "Yeah, how about that time we camped near Moab in Utah as a family? We spent a night on the Colorado River, didn't we?"

"Why yes, we did, great example! What do you remember about the river? Do you remember the river being loud?"

Nyles replied, "No, I don't even remember it making a sound. In fact, I remember feeling relaxed and at ease in the cool shade of the willow trees on the bank."

"It was relaxing. And the river didn't make a sound," said Grandpa. "It was silent, but at the same time immensely powerful! Silent, consistent rivers are responsible for some of the most dramatic and beautiful geographic features on the planet. Think about the Grand Canyon and how it was formed."

Nyles sat there and contemplated what his G-Pa had told him. He then smiled and said, "I hear what you are saying! Every day, silent rivers change the face of the Earth, and in the same way this 'Silent River' can be powerful. I don't have to be loud to create positive change in the world, but I do need to find a way to be heard."

G-Pa grabbed Nyles's hand and said, "I love it, take ownership of the nickname! You are truly a powerful 'Silent River' if I do say so myself!"

"Dinner is ready!" Nyles's mom shouted from the dining room. His conversation with G-Pa had both calmed and recharged him. They sat down and enjoyed the evening meal.

10:50 PM: Nyles's Home

Later, in his bedroom, Nyles was reflecting on the conversation he had with his grandpa. He really liked the idea of "Silent River" being a positive nickname; he just didn't know how he would react the next time someone used it to make fun of him. Nyles grabbed his phone with one hand and started typing a message to Sam with his thumb.

How r u

My grandparents came over tonight and I had a really nice talk with my grandpa

He told me this cool story about my name and my great great g-pa

U mean theres more to it than being named after the nile river

Please tell me more

Maybe if we survive the election

lol

And I cant believe they r giving us tests on monday and tuesday

> **IK**

> Like Im just coming off spending a lot of time preparing for this big speech in front of the whole school and then they go and throw more work at us

Yeah that does kind of suck but at least there r no tests tomorrow or friday

That might have actually been a bad thing because ever since I got home ive just been reading my speech over and over again

I couldve used the distraction

Im gonna try to get some sleep but ill see you tomorrow

Wish me luck and thanks again u r a great friend

"Good luck Sam," Nyles said aloud. "You've got this. I'm the one that needs the luck." Already in the dark, Nyles closed his eyes still thinking about tomorrow, envisioning himself giving his speech. Sleep was going to be a struggle.

Thursday

7:00 AM: Nyles's Home

"Beep! Beep! Beep! Beep!"

Nyles jumped awake, grabbed at his phone, and knocked it off the nightstand.

"Crud," he said as he retrieved his phone and silenced the alarm. He didn't have a great night's sleep, but it had been better than the last couple thanks to his conversation with G-Pa.

Nyles instinctively looked at his messages. His eyes gravitated towards the ones from Sam.

> Morning Nyles

> I believe in u

> Just be yourself

> Youve got this

"I'm still not sure why she didn't ditch me when she had the chance," thought Nyles. As he "heard" himself thinking the negative thought, he immediately mentally countered with, "So much for believing in myself."

He then made the mistake of looking at some of the other texts. Two from the kid that had bumped into him in class stood out.

> Good luck today I heard based on the practice speech youll need it

> U have the right to remain Silent River

"I will never understand why some people have such capacity to hurt others, without so much as a blink of an eye," said Nyles's mother who had quietly entered the room and read the messages from over his shoulder.

"Hey Mom! Not cool!" erupted Nyles.

"Sorry son, but one thing I learned from my career (his mom was a successful business leader at a major investment firm) is that you need to know whose opinion matters. Trust them and ignore those that don't have your best interest at heart. By the way, breakfast is ready. Head on down when you are dressed."

About a half an hour later, Nyles was at the breakfast table. His dad had made an early morning run to Chick-fil-A and picked up one of his favorites, a Hash Brown Scramble Burrito.

"Thanks Dad! What's the occasion?"

"Your mom and I thought you could use a little boost given the stress you have been under," his dad replied. "How are you feeling this morning?"

Nyles's first instinct was to say, "I'm fine," but instead he said, "Truth is I'm stressed. Beyond anxious. I just don't know if I can do this speech today. What if I make a mistake?"

"Where did the courage to say that come from?" Nyles wondered.

"Do you know what one of the most dangerous beliefs that most of us have is?" his dad asked.

Nyles shook his head.

"It's the belief that we must be perfect, or we have failed. I struggled with public speaking for a long time because I thought my delivery had to be perfect. This held me back. What I learned was perfection is a myth. Everyone makes mistakes. Perfection only exists in our minds; we dream up this vision of perfection and then create an expectation that nothing else is acceptable which leads to disappointment. But life isn't perfect. People aren't perfect. Perfection in others isn't really important to people. Do you know what is?"

Once again Nyles shook his head as he took a bite of his breakfast burrito.

"People like authenticity. They appreciate genuineness. They value the truth. Which is great, because that means for most of us all we must do is be ourselves. Embrace those little imperfections that are Nyles, don't fear them. Those are the things that make you unique and memorable."

"Dad, I really wish it were that easy," Nyles replied.

Mom said, "Trust your dad, he knows a thing or two about imperfection." She smiled and winked as she finished her coffee.

7:45 AM: Jane Piety Academy Counselor's Office

Counselor Austin was an early bird. He was almost always the first person in the school office and made a habit of making the first pot of coffee each day. As he was finishing up, he heard a noise and turned around to see Mr. Cobb entering.

"Good morning, Mr. Cobb," said Counselor Austin enthusiastically. "It looks like I'm not the only person who gets here early. I would offer you a fresh cup of coffee, but it isn't quite yet ready."

Mr. Cobb smiled and said, "Thank you. I know I'm a little early. Do you mind if we start ahead of schedule?"

Counselor Austin replied, "No problem, this way into my humble office."

Mr. Cobb entered and immediately noticed that almost every inch of the counselor's office was covered with framed photographs. In addition to the striking contrast to the history classroom, he immediately recognized several places, for example, the Sydney Opera House from an angle that must have been taken from the top of the Sydney

Harbor Bridge!

"I see you like to travel," Mr. Cobb said curiously.

"Yes, I do have a sense of adventure and love to wander our beautiful planet," Counselor Austin answered as he looked around at his photos. "I try to take a big international trip every few years if I can afford it. Two years ago, I traveled to Indonesia and spent some time on Bali and Java. This year I'm headed to the Maldives, I heard the water is pristine and I want to get there before climate change takes a toll and the ocean swallows up the atolls." The counselor smiled at his impromptu tongue twister then continued, "Do you travel?"

Mr. Cobb's facial expression saddened briefly but then he quickly hid his emotions and said, "We traveled some when Margaret was alive, mostly in the desert Southwest of the United States. She loved places like Sedona. I took a leave of absence, and we spent some time there before she lost her battle with cancer. I have been more of a homebody in recent years."

The counselor offered his condolences and there was an awkward pause in the conversation.

Mr. Cobb then proceeded by asking, "Did Mrs. Sweeney talk to you about why I am here?"

Counselor Austin said, "She did stop by for a little while yesterday and gave me a brief overview. Why don't you tell me why you think you're here."

"Sure," said Mr. Cobb. "At first, I didn't really understand what Mrs. Sweeney was talking about. I thought I treated everyone the same, how could I be biased? In fact, I thought that my behavior was an example of non-biased behaviors. But I tried to keep an open mind and yesterday in class I asked the students what I could do to make our discussions more productive. To be honest, I didn't get much new information from the session. In fact, it kind of reaffirmed my perspective. But toward the end of class, I asked Nyles River to speak. As usual, he struggled and talked about needing more time to think, which I dismissed as an excuse. The bell rang so I gave them an assignment to email some suggestions."

Mr. Cobb cleared his throat then said, "Later that day, I received Nyles's ideas. As much as I wanted to dismiss them, they made sense. But it was his final comment that really woke me up. He asked me to stop using an accent when I read his name during attendance. My first reaction was 'what accent?' But then I thought about it, and he was right. Every time I call out his name, I use an accent. And I don't do this with anyone else. Perhaps what is even more disturbing is that even though I knew I was doing it, I never considered how harmful it was to Nyles. It made me think that there very well could be something to Mrs. Sweeney's thoughts on unconscious bias."

Counselor Austin looked up from the notebook he had been scribbling in and said, "Bias, both conscious and unconscious, is normal and is experienced by everyone. It isn't always a bad thing, but when we use it to unfairly treat one person or group differently than the others it can have significant negative consequences."

"It was never my intention to hurt anyone," Mr. Cobb said abruptly.

Counselor Austin responded, "Most people don't realize when they're doing it and never intend harm, but as leaders we must understand that intent isn't near as important as impact. And to your earlier point, you can treat every student the same and still create headwinds that make it harder for some while simultaneously creating tailwinds that make it easier for others.[6] I think that is what Mrs. Sweeney was saying, if your behaviors create a culture that favor the part of your class that leans extroverted, it will be easier for them while at the same time your introverted students will struggle because the nature of the work is harder for them."

He went on to say, "The key is creating a culture that leverages the strengths of everyone, in this case both introverted and extroverted students. You can't treat everyone the same, because of the simple fact that everyone is not the same. You can't ignore either group's needs. And when we as teachers can create a classroom culture that includes students without them having to fit a stereotype, students will finally feel like they belong. They'll be happier and more productive. They'll learn more."

"That does make sense," said Mr. Cobb. "Change is hard. I realize now that I need to make some adjustments. I just hope I'm up to the task."

Counselor Austin smiled again, "I think you will do fine. Please remember you are not alone, and I would be happy to continue to discuss needed changes with you including auditing some of your classes. But before we get that far, I think you probably owe Mr. River an apology for the use of the accent."

Mr. Cobb somehow smiled and frowned simultaneously then said, "Yes, I do!" as he stood up and shook the counselor's hand before exiting the worldly office.

2:40 PM: Jane Piety Academy Auditorium

"Thump-thump... Thump-thump... Thump-thump."

Nyles's heart beat quickly and loudly. His world seemed to close in on him, narrowing his vision. He could feel a weird numbing sensation in his hands and a tightening in his chest. "What is wrong with me?" he thought.

Just then, a deafening roar and thunderous applause erupted from the crowd of students in the auditorium, bringing Nyles back to focus. Mark, Sam's challenger for student council president, was giving his speech.

"Why do we have to wear uniforms?" Mark confidently belted out and in response the students once again screamed and applauded in support.

"Why can't we leave campus for lunch?" More applause and shouts.

"Why don't we have our own Starbucks on campus?" Mark barely got this one out and it felt like the roof of the auditorium might collapse!

He paused, then said "Elect me, Mark Wallace, your next student council president and you'll no longer be asking

'Why!'"

The students rose and applauded in unison. Mark waived, stood there for what seemed like an eternity, then turned and smirked at Sam before returning to his seat.

Nyles worried to himself, "How am I ever going to follow that?!?" He wiped his numb, sweaty, and slightly shaking hands on his uniform shorts.

Mrs. Sweeney walked to the podium. "Thank you Mark for your enthusiastic speech. Now, Nyles River (a few laughs and smirks bubbled up from the audience when she said his name) will introduce our next candidate for student council president. Nyles, the stage is yours." Mrs. Sweeney looked toward Nyles and walked back to her seat.

Nyles felt like his knees would buckle, but he was able to stand and hesitantly made his way toward the podium where, with slightly shaking hands, he opened the binder that contained his speech (a suggestion from Counselor Austin to hide his hand tremors) and placed it on the podium. The mic screeched as he accidentally hit it and the crowd moaned in response.

Nyles looked out over the crowd. Even with the bright

lights, he could see so many faces looking back. He turned his head toward Sam. She sat there with a smile and gave him two thumbs up, which provided a momentary respite from the turmoil he was feeling inside. Every fiber of his being was telling him this was a bad idea, to run and not look back. But he stood there, looking between the students and his speech.

"I can't hear you Silent River!" shouted someone from the back of the crowd.

Nyles couldn't tell who had heckled him. The statement caused the crowd to laugh. Nyles's heart beat faster...

"What is wrong with you dude?!?" yelled another person from the same general area as the first.

This time, a teacher nearby reprimanded the student.

"Indeed, what is wrong with me?" thought Nyles but then he remembered his recent talk with his G-Pa and tried to own the nick name and picture himself as a strong silent river working to change the world forever. He also thought back to his talk with Counselor Austin. Remembering the counselor's advice, Nyles took three slow, deep breaths, looked down and closed his speech.

Mark mumbled just loud enough for Sam to hear, "Here we go again!" Sam grasped the edge of her chair and started to inch forward.

Nyles slowly looked up and before Sam could stand, he started speaking.

"The answer to your question, what is wrong with me, is nothing. There is nothing wrong with me or any of the other students in this school. Often, our culture, beliefs, customs, and everyday behaviors tell a different story though. We learn in a place where bias and discrimination are often accepted and encouraged. In a school where the students that prefer to think about things before they speak about them are considered broken and given daily instruction on how to fix their personalities. In a place where it is common to hear the words 'what is wrong with you' so much that you start to repeat them in your own mind, and worse yet, believe them.

"We learn in an environment where normal is defined as the popular, outgoing person. And we forget that personality type is not defined by one student. It is represented across the student body and it takes every person's unique personality to create a normal distribution of behaviors. Is it so hard to believe that we are all normal? Yes, you heard me correctly, whether you are a student that prefers solitude or one that stands on the lunch table and shouts to everyone that can hear, you are all normal.

"I had prepared a speech to introduce Sam, my closest friend. But, in this moment I decided to scrap it.

"Why, do you ask? Mark asked a lot of 'Why' questions." A few laughs spontaneously popped from the audience. "I have a few of my own.

"Why...why did I choose to throw out my prepared remarks? Because it is time for change. It is time to throw out the familiar and do something new and different. It is time for us to believe in our authentic selves and embrace belonging. We need to stop forcing people to fit in to be successful.

"Why do we choose to call each other names and belittle each other? Perhaps the answer is that our current culture tolerates and even teaches this behavior. So much so that even the recipients often feel it is normal and deserved. A truly sad reality.

"Why am I up here today speaking to you when every fiber

of my being is telling me not to? Because I believe in Sam. I know Sam is the leader we need to make our school better; the leader that will help us see bias and end discrimination. She is a person who lifts others up, not pushes them down. Sam has a kind spirit and believes not only in herself, but in her friends, fellow students, and teachers. She believed in this 'Silent River' so much that she stuck with me when she knew I was struggling with this speech.

"Once again, there is nothing wrong with me and there is nothing wrong with you, but there is something wrong with our current culture and system. Please join me in supporting and electing a person who can lead us in a different direction. Please join me in welcoming our new student council president, Sam Silversmith!"

Nyles turned to Sam and smiled as the students remained silent. She just sat there, looking a bit stunned. Then a person in the back row started applauding, then another, and another and a few others, and soon the entire audience was clapping and standing to welcome Sam to the podium.

Sam stood and started walking toward Nyles who was headed back to his seat. As they passed Nyles let out a big deep breath. Sam gently smiled and reached up to touch his shoulder.

Nyles sat down and worried to himself, "What did I just do? I hope I didn't screw this up for Sam!"

6:00 PM: Nyles's Home

After all the stress from preparing for, worrying about, and then giving the speech, Nyles was in desperate need of alone time. He had cast his vote and then immediately headed home. He went straight to his room and closed the door. Nyles flopped on his bed, silenced his phone, and quickly fell asleep.

He awoke to a gentle knock on the door. It was his mother.

"Nyles, dinner is ready, and you probably shouldn't sleep too long, or you won't sleep tonight," she said through the crack in the door.

"Thanks, Mom," he managed to voice through his dry mouth. "I'll be down in a couple of minutes."

Upon arriving downstairs, Nyles could smell his favorite take-out, Kung Pao Chicken from the Golden Dragon.

His dad looked up from his phone and said, "We know you have had a tough week and thought you would enjoy a good meal!"

"I'll never turn down food from the Golden Dragon!" Nyles enthusiastically said as his mom took her seat at the table. They all served themselves and enjoyed the treat.

As they were nearing the end of the meal, Nyles's mom asked, "How did your and Sam's speeches go today?"

This brought Nyles back to reality. An uneasy feeling returned to his stomach. He looked down and said, "It did not go as planned. I mean, Sam knocked it out of the park, but my introduction was the part that didn't go as I had envisioned in my mind."

His dad said, "I'm sure you did a fine job. Do you want to talk about it?"

Nyles said, "Want to, no. Need to, yes. The thing is, I think I may have messed it up for Sam."

It was Nyles's mom's turn. "Honey, if you spoke from the heart then you have nothing to worry about."

Nyles smiled and replied, "That's just it. At the last possible second, I scrapped the speech that I had been practicing all week and just said what came to my mind. In fact, I'm not sure exactly what I said. But I did get applause, although it was a bit delayed. I headed home right after the speech without talking to anyone. We don't find out the results until tomorrow."

They all sat there silent for a while, then his dad said, "You two up for walking down to that Italian place on the corner for some gelato?"

His mom quickly said, "I would love some! It always reminds me of that place we used to go in New Orleans.

You know that little stand in the French Quarter. You up for it, Nyles?"

Even though he wasn't, he agreed and thought, "At least it will keep me from worrying about the election a little longer."

They got up, cleaned up the dining room and kitchen and then headed out the front door.

7:30 PM: Nyles's Home

It was late evening when Nyles returned home with his parents. He headed upstairs where he had left his phone before dinner. He put it up to his face and unlocked it. It opened and to his surprise he had no less than fifty text messages. Nyles's imagination quickly led him to think, "Oh crud, this can't be good. Someone probably filmed my speech and now I'm viral!"

He hesitantly opened his message and email apps. To his surprise, he had notes from students and teachers, many that he had never contacted before.

Dude, what the heck!

"Not a great start," thought Nyles, but he continued to read.

> Great speech today

> Nyles loved your thoughtful honesty today your speech made a lot of people think

> SR, keep the words flowing

> Why!?!

> Nyles, way to go dude! You want to write my next speech for me? I'll pay you!!!!!

> Until I heard your speech today, I always thought I was alone. My family doesn't get me, my teachers don't, and I've had a hard time finding close friends. Thank you so very much for opening my eyes. With silent solidarity, Ruby K.

And on they went, they were all positive, at least they could all be interpreted positively. Nyles continued to scroll through the messages and emails. There was one from Mr. Austin, a couple from Mrs. Sweeney, and even one from Mr. Cobb that read, "Mr. River, outstanding speech today. I underestimated you." Scroll. Scroll. Scroll. Then he saw the text he was looking for, from Sam.

> Nyles, u left so quickly after the speech we didnt get a chance to talk

> U nailed it

> Your introduction was amazing

> I knew u were the right person for the job

> Thank u so much and we will talk more tomorrow at our victory celebration

Nyles thought, "Our victory celebration, don't you mean yours?" Then he noticed that the weight of the world had been lifted from his shoulders. The anxiety and stress he had been carrying all week had evaporated. Nyles laid back on his pillow and fell fast asleep.

Friday

7:00 AM: Nyles's Home

"Beep! Beep! Beep! Beep!"

Slowly, Nyles opened his eyes and peeked out from under his pillow. "Man, that was a great night's sleep!" he thought.

Nyles let the alarm continue to beep while he relived yesterday's speech and positive feedback. Finally, he reached over and hit snooze. He deserved a few more minutes.

Twenty minutes later, he awoke to the sound of his mom yelling from the bottom of the stairs.

"Nyles! Nyles! Nyles!"

"Shoot!" Nyles thought. "I've overslept!"

Thankfully, Anxiety High required uniforms, so not much thought had to go into getting dressed. Even though today was a free dress day because of tonight's football game, Nyles quickly donned his gray shorts, white Polo pullover shirt and his nondescript athletic shoes. Mark had talked about eliminating uniforms in his campaign speech, but uniforms were something Nyles liked about school. It was the one thing about Anxiety High that actually reduced anxiety.

He ran downstairs, grabbed his computer, homework, and books, and quickly shoved everything into his backpack.

"Morning Nyles," his dad yelled from the kitchen. "What do you want for breakfast?"

"Morning Dad!" Nyles yelled back. "Thanks, but nothing. I'll grab something from the cafeteria." He hoisted his heavy backpack on his shoulder and kissed his mom's waiting cheek as he hurried out the front door and off to school.

8:00 AM: Jane Piety Academy Cafeteria

Nyles grabbed a quick Southwestern breakfast burrito and an OJ and found an empty table. Soon Sam joined him, foregoing breakfast because she was still nervous about the yet-to-be announced election results.

"I can't eat, my stomach is in knots!" she said.

"You've got this, your speech was great! People loved it!" Nyles mumbled through a mouth full of burrito.

"You're disgusting!" Sam joked. "But thank you I really appreciate it. And thanks for yesterday. I know it wasn't easy for you."

About that time their friend Johnny showed up with a girl named Ruby Knoll "Hey guys, can we join you?" asked Johnny. "Do ya'll know Ruby?" Ruby waved as her eyes drifted down.

Sam said, "Of course, we've all been at this school for several years and have had multiple classes together."

Nyles pulled out an extra chair and motioned for Ruby to sit. Still chewing, Nyles said to Ruby, "Thanks for the text message last night. It really lifted my spirits. I bet it took some courage to send it. And, believe me, you're not alone!"

Ruby grinned, looked down again and said, "You're welcome." Her eyes slowly rose to meet his., "No one understands me, not even my family. Your speech really helped me see, for the first time, that there are others struggling in similar ways. So, thanks."

Ignoring their side conversation, Johnny laughed and said, "Did you see that new video of the cat that head butted the glass every time a bird landed outside on the window ledge? Don't worry, the cat was fine. It just shook its head and went about its business. It's got like a million views." They all joined in the needed distraction.

8:30 AM: Jane Piety Academy History Class

Nyles narrowly slipped through the history classroom's door just milliseconds prior to the first period bell and quickly found his seat.

Mr. Cobb was sitting at his desk. "OK people, please quiet down."

The noise of the combined students' voices slowly died down until it was almost quiet, except for Linsey who, when she realized she was the only one still talking quickly stopped and apologized.

Mr. Cobb looked at Linsey and said, "No need to apologize Miss Lopez. In fact, it is I who is the one who should be apologizing."

The students were caught off guard. Not one of them had ever heard Mr. Cobb apologize for anything, especially not to a student. The room remained quiet.

"But before I do, let me complete the roll call," said Mr. Cobb as he looked down at his gradebook.

Nyles thought, "Why should this history class be any different?" and waited for Mr. Cobb's strange accent when he called his name. Mr. Cobb began and continued methodically calling names and waiting for the standard reply "...Noah Oliver...Here...June Peterson...Here...James Payton...Here...Nyles River...Here..."

"Wait!" Nyles thought as the roll call continued. "He didn't use the accent today! Nobody laughed! What just happened?"

After finishing attendance, Mr. Cobb stood and walked to the front of his desk. "As I was saying, I owe you an apology. You see, over the past few days my eyes have been opened to my own personal unconscious biases. Thanks to some sobering feedback from a few of my peers and students, I have come to realize that although it wasn't my intention, I have created and reinforced a classroom culture that was not welcoming to many of you. One of the things about bias that I have learned, is that it is often easy to see it in others, but extremely hard to see in yourself. The feedback that I received helped me look clearly in the mirror and examine some of my beliefs and behaviors. I realize that I need to change. So that is what is going to happen, I'm going to start working to make my classroom one where everyone, regardless of who you are or where you come from, feels like they belong."

Nyles was in shock. He looked around and the feeling apparently was shared by many others based on the number of open mouths he counted.

"Nyles," said Mr. Cobb. He didn't need to be prompted more than once this time; he was in the moment. "I would like to start by apologizing to you. My use of that strange accent to introduce you was inappropriate, not funny, and I am embarrassed that I engaged in such behavior. It will not happen again. My hope is that you will be able to forgive me and that this class can be one where you find joy and look forward to attending."

Nyles nodded and Mr. Cobb nodded in return.

"Next," continued Mr. Cobb, "I would like to apologize to my students that lean to the introverted side of the personality type spectrum. I have recently come to realize that my teaching techniques, although consistent for all, really benefited the more extroverted students. From now on, our classroom activities will be more balanced between speaking and writing and your grades will not be overly weighted to public speaking. To be clear, if you are introverted you will still be expected to stretch yourself on occasion and work outside your comfort zone just like the students who are more naturally outgoing will be expected to stretch themselves on the assignments that are more tailored to the introverted students."

A hand went up.

"Yes Mr. Oliver," said Mr. Cobb.

Noah dropped his hand and asked, "What is extroverted and introverted?"

Mr. Cobb looked down, smiled, and said, "Great question. Simply put, introverts gain energy in quiet, low stimulus environments and lose it in settings where there are high levels of stimulation, like in crowds. The opposite is true for extroverts. All personality types are normal, and no one personality type is better than the other. I think I'll have Counselor Austin come in and give us a more in-depth overview of personality type. Thank you for asking."

Mr. Cobb concluded, "With that said, plus given the excitement around the election results and tonight's football game, I am going to dismiss class early today." He expected the students to cheer, but to his surprise they remained silent. "I mean it, get out before I change my mind," he said with a smile.

Students quickly started packing their bags and soon the classroom was empty except for Nyles and Mr. Cobb.

"Thanks Mr. Cobb, I really appreciate what you did today," said Nyles as he walked toward the door.

Mr. Cobb replied, "It was really a great speech yesterday. You should be proud. It had a positive impact on me, and I know it did on many others."

Nyles looked at the history teacher and nodded; Mr. Cobb nodded back then Nyles left the room. This time his heart was beating fast from excitement, not anxiety.

12:30 PM: Jane Piety Academy Cafeteria

"Hey Nyles, over here!" someone shouted from across the cafeteria. He scanned the room and saw Sam waiving. She was sitting alone at a table for two. Nyles nodded since his hands were holding his lunch tray and headed in her direction.

"Any results yet?" Nyles asked Sam as he sat down at the small table, bumping it and almost spilling Sam's drink.

She smiled and said, "I know the result, but Mrs. Sweeney swore me and Mark to secrecy until they announce, which should be soon."

"Come on, it is just me. I won't tell anyone," replied Nyles with a wink. Just as Sam leaned over to whisper to him, static came out over the school intercom system.

"Attention student body," Mrs. Sweeney's voice echoed from the ceiling speakers. "I have the results of yesterday's student council president elections. Please join me in congratulating your new president, Sam Silversmith!" There was a healthy round of applause from the cafeteria and Sam smiled and waved to a few supporters who were seated close by. Mrs. Sweeney continued to announce the results but was drowned out by the crowd as the students generally went about visiting and eating.

Nyles offered Sam a huge high five, which she enthusiastically returned.

"Congratulations Sam! I'm excited for you and know you'll do a great job," he said.

Sam had a bit of a devilish look on her face. "There is something I think you need to know." Sam leaned in and whispered, "Mrs. Sweeney told me that I got just over fifty percent of the vote compared to Mark's twenty percent."

Nyles offered another high five and said, "Wow, a landslide victory!"

Sam waived off his high five and said, "You're somewhat of a math genius. Don't you want to know where the rest of the votes went?"

Nyles hadn't really thought about it, but thirty percent of the votes were not accounted for in Sam's totals.

"I don't know, they were left blank?" he guessed.

"No silly! I'm going to have to rethink your math genius status. Blank votes are not counted," quipped Sam. "Look, the majority of the remaining students that voted for president wrote a name on the ballot."

Nyles replied, "I didn't know that was a thing."

Sam sighed, "Think about it. Aren't you curious who's name they wrote down?"

As Nyles looked at Sam with some confusion, she saw in his eyes the moment he realized who had received all these mystery votes. Nyles hesitantly said, "They wrote in my... name?"

Sam's smile grew and her eyes widened as she slowly shook her head yes.

6:00 PM: Home

When Nyles came downstairs for dinner, he was surprised

and happy to see his grandpa. "Hey G-Pa, what are you doing here!"

"Just dropping off some things from your grandmother," replied G-Pa.

"Cool!"

"Your Dad said your speech turned out well," G-Pa sort of stated and sort of asked.

"It did," Nyles said. "I won't lie, it was a stressful week, and I wasn't sure I was going to make it, but the talk we had at dinner the other day really helped. Thank you again."

G-Pa smiled. "Any time. You headed to the game tonight?"

"I don't think so." Nyles shrugged. "I don't like being the center of attention and if tonight is anything like today, I'll have a lot of people commenting on my speech. I never really know what to say."

"You want a little more advice?" asked G-Pa.

Nyles smiled and nodded his head in affirmation.

"Go and have fun. When someone pays you a compliment all you need to say is 'thank you.' And if you really want to turn the tables on them, give them a compliment by adding a 'you are so kind' to the end."

Nyles smiled sneakily. "Thank you, G-Pa. You are so kind."

8:00 PM: Jane Piety Academy Football Field

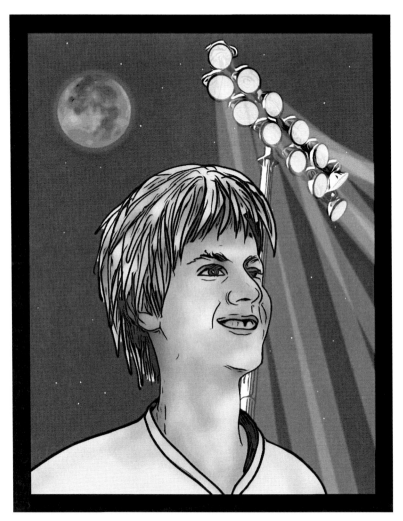

At the game, Nyles met up with Sam and a few other friends. They talked a bit about the election, but the conversation quickly reverted to their usual banter. Occasionally, someone would walk by and yell "Silent

River, you rock" or something similar. The nickname that had been bestowed as a put-down had become a badge of courage that Nyles now wore with pride. As he looked over the field, Nyles felt—for the first time in a long time—that there was nothing wrong with him and that he belonged at Jane Piety Academy.

To be continued in ***Anxiety High Volume 2: You are not Alone!***

Acknowledgements

This book is dedicated to the introverted teens who are struggling to find their way in a world that favors extroverted behaviors. There is nothing wrong with you!

A special thanks to Mary, Zachary, Erica, Chaili, Sydney, Stephen, Cathy, Shawn, Lee, and Joe who helped make this book so special. We dearly appreciate your time, kind considerations, and thoughtful advice.

About the Authors

David and Joshua Boroughs are a father-son writing team from Houston, Texas. David is the author of ***The Extrovert's Guide to Elevating Introverted Leaders in the Workplace***. He is a retired professional engineer and corporate leader now focusing on his family while pursuing his passion as an author and artist. Joshua is a high school student and ***Anxiety High Volume 1: There is Nothing Wrong with You!*** is his first book. He is a typical teenager who spends his spare time with his friends, playing video games, running, and now writing. Both David and Joshua are introverts with a desire to help others learn how to be authentically happy and successful, while simultaneously championing cultural change so people of all personality types feel like they belong.

Notes

[1] In English, the Spanish phrase "gente de color mija" means "people of color my daughter".

[2] In English, the Spanish phrase "ay Dios mio" means "oh my god".

[3] In English, the Spanish word "calmate" means "calm down".

[4] In English, the Spanish phrase "por favor" means "please".

[5] In English, the Spanish phrase "como estas" means "how are you".

[6] "Headwinds" refer to unfair conditions that make it unnecessarily harder for one group to succeed than the other groups. "Tailwinds" refer to conditions that make it unfairly easier for one group to succeed while the other groups do not benefit from the advantage.

Manufactured by Amazon.ca
Acheson, AB